SUITS YOU SIRE!

KING ALBERT-HORATIO-OTTO THE THIRD

KING SNAPS UP SUPER SNIPPERS!

ALL IS REVEALED

MITCH (LEFT) AND McTAVISH

THAT FANTASTIC FABRIC

What We Know So Far...

ARISE!
Sir Mitch & McTavish

EXCLUSIVE
SHOTS OF WONDER WEAVERS

BLOOMSBURY CHILDREN'S BOOKS
Bloomsbury Publishing Plc
50 Bedford Square, London, WC1B 3DP, UK
29 Earlsfort Terrace, Dublin 2, Ireland
BLOOMSBURY, BLOOMSBURY CHILDREN'S BOOKS and
the Diana logo are trademarks of Bloomsbury Publishing Plc
First published in Great Britain 2021 by Bloomsbury Publishing Plc

A catalogue record for this book is available from the British Library

ISBN: HB: 978 1 4088 6013 7

PB: 978 1 4088 6014 4

eBook: 978 1 4088 6015 1

2 4 6 8 10 9 7 5 3 1

Printed in China by Leo Paper Products, Heshan, Guangdong
All papers used by Bloomsbury Publishing Plc are
natural, recyclable products from wood grown
in well managed forests.
The manufacturing processes conform to
the environmental regulations of the country of origin.

To find out more about our authors and books
visit www.bloomsbury.com and sign up for our newsletters

For Theo and Tara.
Good things come to
those who wait – x P.B.

For Simba, who told
me I could when I was
convinced I couldn't – x C.P.

PETER BENTLY   CLAIRE POWELL

The King's Birthday Suit

From the story by Hans Christian Andersen

BLOOMSBURY
CHILDREN'S BOOKS

LONDON OXFORD NEW YORK NEW DELHI SYDNEY

King Albert-Horatio-Otto the Third
had so many clothes it was simply absurd.

He had outfits for yoga
and stroking his cat.

He **never** ate cheese
without changing his hat.

For every event he would wear something new –
he even changed outfits to go to the loo.

"It'll soon be my birthday!" the King said one day.
"There'll be royalty coming from far, far away.
I'll need a new suit, the best there can be.
Who will design a new outfit for me?"

Fashion designers turned up in their droves,

bringing the King all their latest new clothes.

But nothing His Majesty tried was quite right.

"This cloth is too scratchy, and simply too bright!

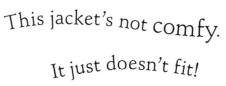

This jacket's not comfy.

It just doesn't fit!

Too stripey and spotty –

I look a right twit!"

Along came two rascals, McTavish and Mitch
who'd cooked up a story to make themselves rich.
"We'll make you a suit of the finest cloth ever,
which can only be seen by the wise and the clever!"

The King said, "Fantastic!
That's just what I need.
I'll make sure you're paid
very highly indeed."

Then Mitch and McTavish pretended to weave
the fabulous fabric from morning till eve.

Clackety-clickety,

clickety-clack.

Working their weaving-loom forward and back.

Clickety-clackety,

clackety-click.

Nobody guessed it was
all a **big trick.**

A day or two later, while changing for tea,
the King had a thought, with a chuckle of glee:
"My ministers think they're a pretty smart lot.
We'll find out who's clever like me – and who's not!"

He ordered his ministers, "Please go and see
my amazing new cloth, and describe it to me."

But the ministers entered
the room in dismay.
They couldn't see *anything*!
What would they say?

They said to the King,
"That cloth, sir – oh my!

We've seen nothing like it!"
(Which wasn't a lie.)

"We just can't describe it!"
they said.
(Which was true.)

"It's quite unbelievable!"
(That was true, too.)

So off went the King, just as pleased as can be,
and he had a great shock – not a thing could he see!

But he said, "Why . . . this cloth is amazing, dear fellows!
It's as light as a feather! And I love all those . . . yellows!"

Next, they pretended to
cut out the suit.
Snip! went their scissors.
Snip-snip! (What a hoot!)

"Your suit," said McTavish,
"will fit like a dream."
"You'll look quite astounding!"
said Mitch. (What a scream!)

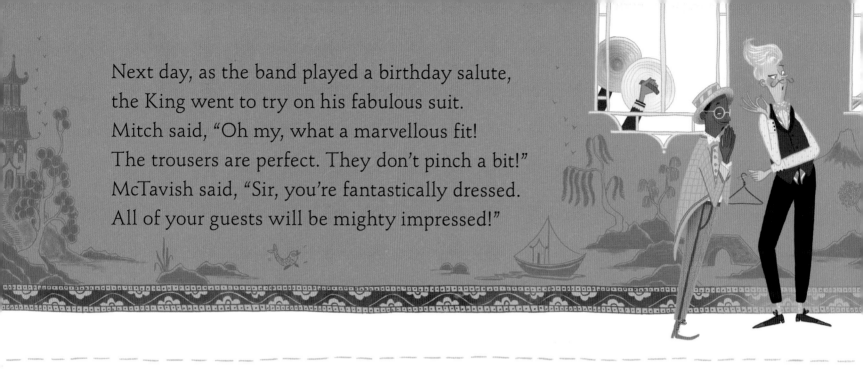

Next day, as the band played a birthday salute,
the King went to try on his fabulous suit.
Mitch said, "Oh my, what a marvellous fit!
The trousers are perfect. They don't pinch a bit!"
McTavish said, "Sir, you're fantastically dressed.
All of your guests will be mighty impressed!"

At the party that evening, the guests gave a cheer
when the butler announced: "His Majesty's here!"

They had all heard the tale of the wonderful clothes,
and they strained for a glimpse on the tips of their toes.

His Majesty haughtily strode into sight . . .
Oh, the King made a mighty impression, all right!

A duchess, who just couldn't stop herself staring,
declared, "What a splendid new outfit he's wearing!"
And all of the guests were quick to agree –
so no one would think they were stupid, you see.

But one little girl stepped out of the crowd,
pointed her finger and hollered out loud:
"You grown-ups are silly! Can't you all see?
The King is STARK NAKED! He's as bare as can be!"

She started to giggle. The others did too –

and the King turned bright red
for he knew it was true.

He turned and marched off the same way he had come . . .

as everyone laughed at the royal . . .

bare bum.

BARE FACED CHEEK

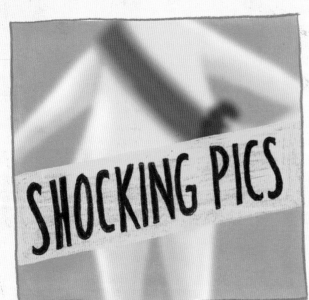

SHOCKING PICS

LIES! LIES! LIES!

THE ROYAL EXPOSÉ!

ALL WAS REVEALED

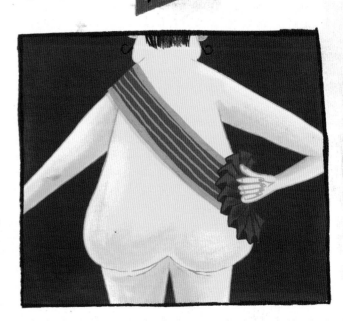

IT'S A RIGHT ROYAL *Stitch Up!*

FABRICATED FABRIC WAS TISSUE OF LIES!

We Told You SEW!